AMMONIAC

Henry Maguire

HYPERIDEAN PRESS

Hyperidean Press
www.hyperideanpress.com

Ammoniac/ Henry Maguire – First Edition October 2025

Edited by Udith Dematagoda and Elliot Burr

Cover: 'Untitled' by Fergus Poglase 2025

ISBN 978-1-9163767-3-1

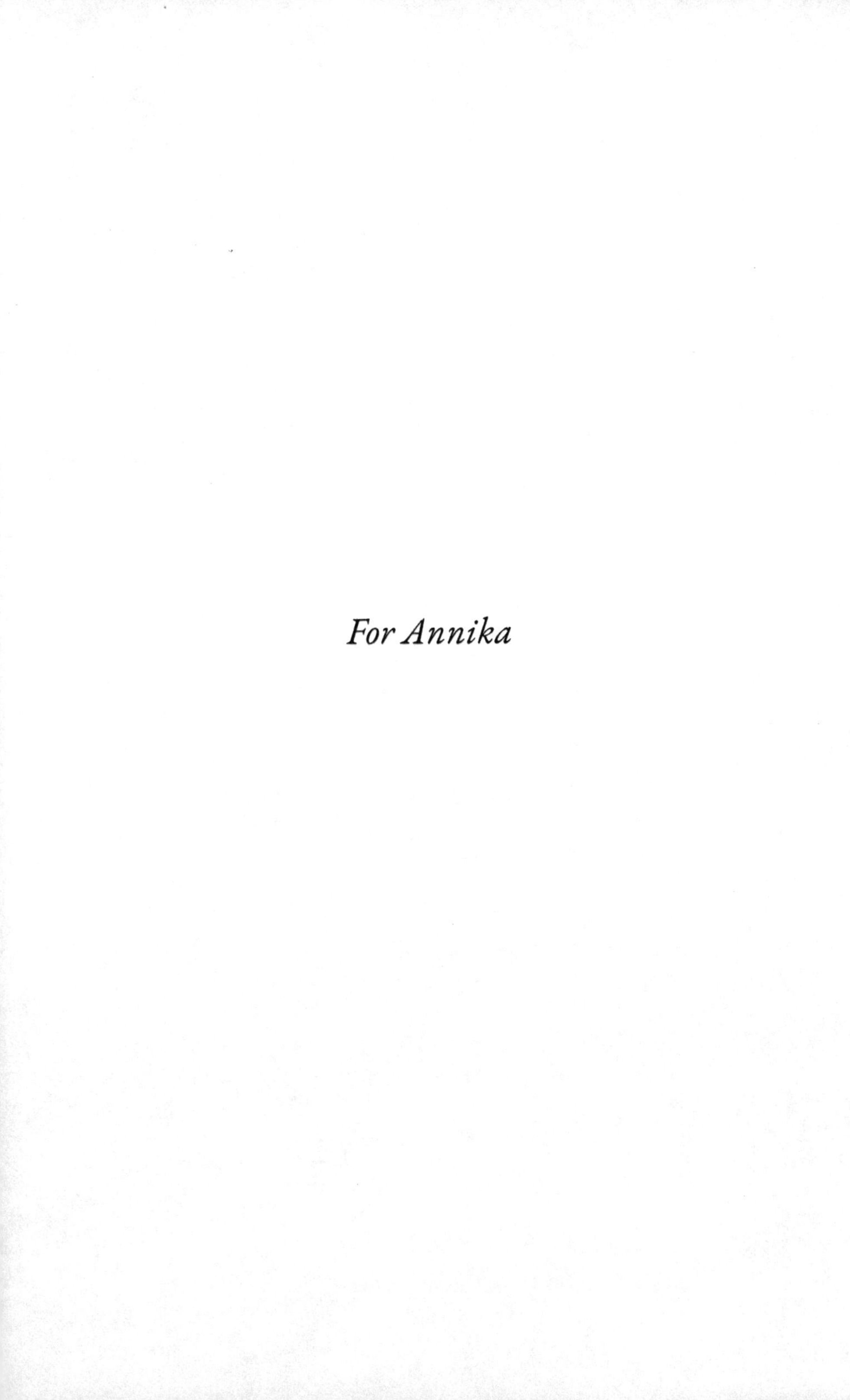

For Annika

I continued in oblivion lost,
My head was resting on my love;
Lost to all things and myself,
And, amid the lilies forgotten,
Threw all my cares away.

\- St. John of the Cross

PA

ONE

RT

1

It takes human cells around seven years to completely replace themselves. That would be a tough stretch of time to kill before I had any concrete evidence that I wasn't the same person anymore. Someone had taken the time to figure out that our current functional unit had a recurring sell-by date. At first I felt doomed. It was a fact: we were always decaying and continuously replaced. That being said, this backdoor deal with nature also gave you several chances at getting it right. As of 2017, the life expectancy in the UK was 81 years old. That gave you roughly eleven goes. This was arguably pretty generous. From this moment here, one that I know will be a fatal place marker, several trillion specks of me will live out their natural lives. They will no doubt do what is expected of them, barring any serious disease or act of God. Then, finally, they will each surrender gently in turn, and melt away to join the great compost heap of dead information. She was already walking ahead, at around ten or so metres in the Père Lachaise Cemetery; the most visited necropolis in the world. She wasn't talking to me anymore, and probably wouldn't do so ever again. In a few years some other painful thing will surely come along and right now will feel like distant, muted agony.

2

I was sitting with my eyes dead on a blue narrow chair at the Jobcentre on the second floor at 24-26 Peckham High Street. I could overhear a young Glaswegian man at the next desk explaining to his Work Coach how he had had to leave his hostel several days previously after being set upon by two crackheads.

'Then see one of them pokes me in the neck with this screwdriver!' he protested, rubbing his nose with the knuckle of his index finger. This was the reason why he had not shown up for his last appointment. I scanned his neck for any marks. My work coach was trying to get my attention.

'Do you want me to repeat the last one?'

'Uh, yeah,'

She was an Indian woman in her mid fifties called Tanu, stern but kind-eyed to the right answers. I had been with her before but she didn't remember me. She leaned closer to her computer monitor, adjusted her glasses, and continued reading off of a Council Tax Reduction form.

'Have you ever received a Far Eastern Prisoners of War compensation payment?'

I looked at her blankly.

'No,'

'Have you received a compensation payment made to the victims of the atrocities that happened during the Second World War?'

'The Second World War?'

'It's on the form.'

I thought about whether I could get away with describing my life as an atrocity. In part, I wished it was interesting enough. I smiled to myself; my capacity for internal pomp seemed to know no bounds. I ultimately regarded my life as a mediocre and uneventful one, despite any minor personal achievements that would offer the briefest distractions of pride or hope. Sooner or later, I would always come back down to the understanding that I led a softcore, whitewash, baby shit existence – I felt very conventional.

'No,' I replied.

I looked out the window behind Tanu at the budget supermarket car park below. There would be a future, one in which reactionary naked ape archeologists delicately excavated vapes with electric toothbrushes. It may be one that would hold these to be fascinating times, but the truth was that they bored me shitless. Tanu leaned back in her tippy chair.

'I've referred you to the Job Entry Targeted Support team.'

She pushed a colourful leaflet across the desk. The front cover had a girl in a hijab and a white buttoned down shirt, sitting at a laptop in a brightly lit, antiseptic office. There were huge glass windows behind her with a skyline view and a plant that was out of focus on the desk. I opened up the leaflet. Inside, the girl was standing up with her arms outstretched like in Titanic. Underneath the copy read:

THERE'S NOTHING TO LOSE...
JUST A WHOLE WORLD OF WORK TO GAIN

'They will contact you sometime in the next two days.'

I gave her a pitiful smile, folded the leaflet and placed it into my jacket pocket.

3

I came home to find Lawrence sitting at the kitchen table in his boxers and eating an entire rotisserie chicken with his bare hands. Lawrence was obese and had more hair on his shoulders than on his head. I think he was a lorry driver. This was the first time that I had seen him out of his hi-vis overalls. It felt like I was interrupting a tender moment; hunched forward and molesting the thing, he was chewing on skin and sucking his fingers. A fat man taken off death row.

'Alright,' I said.

'Got this whole fucking thing reduced,' It had been a good day for Lawrence.

'Don't hurt yourself.'

I went upstairs to my room and lay down on the bed, opened up a 35cl of own-brand gin, took a swig, and looked at the wall. I had quit drinking for around three months earlier in the summer. I didn't see myself as an alcoholic, but I had come across a more modern spectral diagnosis of "alcohol use disorder" that was difficult to disprove. This uncharacteristic bout of sobriety had not worked. That is to say, nothing had been achieved in those months of clarity. If anything, they had only gotten worse. In recent weeks, the wagon I had been on had transformed into a shopping trolley, dumped and algae-submerged in a canal; wagons, I had decided, were only driven by high horses anyway. It seemed I was able to go an average of thirteen days without too much discomfort, but any longer than that and some trigger always had to be pulled, one that I have never fully been able to understand. Perhaps I did not possess the appropriate reflective practices. Seemingly without fail, around this time, conditions were met and some mental reset was required; a sort of bored, restless detonation.

The night before, I had finally gotten around to framing a poster that had been close to my heart for several years. It was now wall-mounted, and behind what Amazon describes as "Safe Perspex, in a MODERN BLACK 12 x 16 INCH FRAME". The poster is an A3 topless photograph of page 3 girl-turned-kids' TV presenter, Gail McKenna. She was in *The Sun* from '86-90 before being born again and finding spiritual rebirth at *CITV*. Looking at it now, I am taken by the moment and begin extensively googling GAIL MCKENNA TITS for around six minutes. I gave up on page 11 and considered deleting my browsing history. The drop-down menu on Chrome offers multiple options for achieving this, enabling the user to censor their sexuality to varying degrees; it becomes apparent that your shame can be determinable, as a measurement of time. You may choose from: the last hour, the last 24 hours, the last seven days, the last four weeks, or the ultimate nuclear winter of all time. I contemplated masturbating. My door was still open, and my eye was drawn to a mouse, slowly crawling down the hall. It must have been injured. They were normally pretty spritely, but this one was just dragging itself along, spreading its guts all over Omaha Beach. An exterminator had been around the week before.

'Two things to remember son,' he had said. 'Mice can't resist a hole, and cheese is just a fallacy. After they munch on a bit of this, they stagger around pissed like for a bit, then it's game over.' I remembered the receipt he had left. It was still on my desk on muted grey paper. There was a list of maybe a dozen or so poisons in a checkbox, followed by the date on which it had been distributed. Now here the poor thing was, not having the best time of it; on his way towards his little oblivion – off his little head on NeoSorexa. Ten minutes later I went into the bathroom, and as I pissed, looked down out the window to the neighbours' patio. These people, it seemed, were forever ready for a summer. A table set out with a permanent spread, despite any weather. The funtime display was held all year round, rain or shine. There was always an abundance of cheap Czech bottled beer and knock-off mini Pringles. Next to the table there lay a kicked-in pedal bin – car parts and headlights littered the mossy concrete. Empty jars lay underneath the table with coloured lids, all amongst an assortment of pesticides; the camping chairs were always left set out with brimming ash-trayed cup holders. I returned to my room and sank into the desk chair. "Jockey Full Of Bourbon" came on through my headphones. I closed my eyes and sucked in my lower lip and hunched forward; tapping my knees and swaying my shoulders to the double bass, I decided that I would fare perfectly well in a Cuban jail. The TV was a few feet away. At 40inches it was definitely too large for the space. It had been broken for a few weeks; a single knuckle crack was present on the top left of the screen. It had remained on its stand, like a fat black obelisk, drawing in a sustained void from the room. This must have been my motive for the assault. I sat down at my desk and looked at what was left there. A piece of yellow lined paper pissing through with dried red wine read:

"The human animal will demand answers to questions that are perhaps better let be,

he will never be satisfied without overturning every rock, yet he himself lives under immovable objects."

It took six hours of drinking to produce this piece of wank, and I had no clue what it was supposed to mean.

4

The next morning I was woken by a call. Sunlight crept in through the blinds; traffic crawled around outside.

'Good morning! This is Anuj from the Job Entry Targeted Support team, how are you today?'

The voice was American, energetic and insincere. He must have been screaming on the inside. Had he psyched himself up for this call? It must have been hard to maintain such enthusiasm on the phone with God knows how many unemployable retards a day.

'I'm fine.' I got up and wandered over to the desk and sat down, two pins nestled in the chair's armrest. I took each out in turn and stuck them back in again, over and over.

'The reason for my call today is to have a quick conversation just to give you an introduction to our services. Did you have a chance to look over the materials given to you by your Work Coach?'

The leaflet was still on the desk, though the top half of the front cover had been repeatedly roached, beheading the hijab girl. I opened it to some copy on the left-hand side that read:

RETURNING TO WORK: THE 4 P's OF SUCCESS

Personal Care (Self care, routine and support)

Positive Action (Positive thinking/reframing and setting goals)

Practical Steps (Effective telephone skills, updating CV, upskilling, attending workshops)

Proactive (Applying for jobs, approaching employers, volunteering)

'Sure, they're right here.'

'Well I'll just leave you to get acquainted with the information and I will call you again in a week to see how you're getting on with your work search. In the meantime, we will email you exclusive positions that aren't listed elsewhere. You have a good day now.' Exclusive. He had said it. Perhaps

I had made it – golden handshakes, grubby deals. I sat there on my phone and went on autopilot. There were numerous unread email alerts for jobs. I had had a job some weeks before, in a pretty dead pub. The manager had told me that I had to ask before going for a piss and I just walked straight out of there. Oh well. I would be skint. I knew that the Universal Credit shitstorm would be coming. But I knew how to go to ground; I'd done it before, and I would do it again. No doubt. The most recent alert in the inbox jumped out in bold threatening letters:

KITCHEN PORTER (MATERNITY COVER)

I thought of the Virgin Mother, heavily pregnant, her huge Messiah bulge spilling over into a gastropub sink. Her water breaking over her bare feet, whilst she jet-sprayed ketchup out of ramekins. After years of menial jobs, mainly in bars, I had learnt that taking the piss was an art form – it took time to develop the skill. You had to give the impression that it was handled while getting away with whatever you could under the table. Once a lad called Jim and I had run a scam where we sold our own bottles of beer from the ASDA. We somehow managed to clear £300 a week for six weeks before anyone noticed. If you didn't try and pull something then it was literally killing time with nothing to show for it other than minimum wage, and that truly scared me. I had looked up the definition of the 'Living Wage', i.e "enough to maintain a normal standard of living". Some cunt asking me to attempt to throw out a maniac or to clean the sick and shit off the walls expected me to do so willingly in order to secure a sub-par quality of life and be grateful for it. Early on I started to see the job market as a hostage-taker. I read up on crisis negotiation – specifically something called the Behavioural Change Stairway Model. This supposedly involved five steps: active listening, empathy, rapport, influence and, ultimately, behavioural change. I began using the strategy in interviews and it worked like a charm. I could create the illusion of the responsible, subordinate worker, dependable and with plenty of *get up and go*. I would demonstrate enthusiasm for the business, drive and capability for the workload, but most importantly, a faint tint of financial desperation. But before long my attitude would cave. Around the same time as I walked out on my last job, my life undoubtedly changed. I had been hungover and eating a newsagent samosa while crossing the Caledonian Road when I had a fatal realisation. I had become aware of a truth that rooted itself in my mind like meat in teeth. It was this truth that I now knew would accompany every waking thought and leer over any attempt at action. The thought was simple: that I was going to die and there wasn't a thing I could do about it. Now, I had always known this; dying wasn't new or particularly relevant information, it was just something I had never believed in before, like National Insurance. I had been distracted. There was much that distracted me. But that didn't seem to matter as much anymore. Now I truly knew, like cancer in my mind, that I was going to die. When it came down to it, there was no miraculous thing about me; I was not the clever exception. I was nothing in particular and now truly understood that there was no way I could do this forever. A few moments before, back on the other side of the road, my mind had been younger. I had seen myself as a dreamer. Dreams had sat there in my head for years, comfortable and reassuring. But now, in an instant, it was all over. I knew that they weren't getting any closer, and I had begun to wonder just how long I was meant to tolerate a life without them.

5

In the afternoon I went over to *The Joiners Arms* on Denmark Hill. I had managed to get a solid short story out of working there a year before and it was one of the only places where my tenure as a bartender had ended somewhat amicably. I'm not sure if I count it as being sacked; they just stopped asking me to come in for work. That didn't stop me from coming in every now and again to sit and rot. To get served quickly, one must make oneself cordially unavoidable. I ordered a pint of 1664 and made my way over to the back room where it was marginally more private. Spotting a four seater with "reserved for Callum, 3:30pm" written in nice hand on a piece of off-white paper, tied with string to an empty bottle of Laphroaig, I sat down to drink. I felt sorry for Callum, trying to get me off this table in an hour and a half. I pulled out a small red notebook and started writing about the roadkill I'd seen earlier on. It was the most gruesome thing that I had ever seen, and I stared at it for some time. It looked like it had been a fox. The skull was split into two jagged pieces and the brains were laid out in chum. It was unlike the more noble badgers you tended to see in the countryside, underneath the brief glow of headlights, splayed on their back, having been dragged to the side of the lane to rest away from the indignity of a double yellow line. A young father, having finished his permitted two pints, exits with a buggy and his missus. Not even half a buzz on, he looks back towards the bar after getting so close to feeling beautiful. I went out the front to smoke. In the doorway I stood and fingered the corner of a 30g pouch of Gold Leaf. I had to start rolling them slim. Everything within reason would now have to be limited; a life downsized. I couldn't believe it – I was becoming a bean counter. The paper came together awkwardly in a palsy origami.

An uncomfortable stand-off on one of the tables between a man and a woman was underway beside me. The man, having asked to sit next to her, was met with a frozen glance. He recoiled and before she could respond, reassured her he was waiting for his wife, with a tilting head gesture towards a half pint to prove it. Then to the right was a pair of particularly unspectacular looking friends. 'So... how's being a line manager working out?' One asked the other. I put out my cigarette before it was finished and went back inside.

Back in the pub, the football had been turned on, routine for the afternoons. This time though, it was the women's. Two old heads in flat caps looked up at the screen, one let out a groan while the other shook his head.

'What's next?!' I said to a mumbled jeer of approval on my way back to the bar. Before I could order, a heavy set black man burst through the door. He began pacing around.

'Two kids just tried to mug me mate,'

There was no one else at the bar. He must have been addressing me.

'Oh yeah?' I tried not to give away too much.

'Yeah two little cunts. I say to them, Hey if there's two of you then I'm allowed to fucking break something, you know what I mean?'

'Sounds fair.'

'NIGGLETS, THAT'S WHAT THEY ARE. FUCKING NIGGLETS!'

He sort of calmed down after that, ordered a double gin and tonic. Molly, the bar girl who had been there before me, placed the gin and a bottle of tonic on the bar. He ignored the tonic completely, downed the thing in one, and left.

'That was a quick one' she laughed.

Sweet Molly. Over time she had been anaesthetised to the many waves of the unhinged that popped in just to say hello. I couldn't tell if she was thick or not.

'Where you working at now then?'

Fuck her for bringing that up.

'Never again, I can't stand the pubs anymore'

'Then why do you still come in here?'

'I'm alright sitting on this side.'

'And what's happened to your head?'

I stroked my left temple. I had a small bump. It was some kind of haematoma, a lump of congealed blood from a pretty good right hook I had taken on Greek Street a week earlier. I don't remember a thing. I had woken up with no marks on my knuckles or palms to indicate that I broke a fall or that things had gone too far on my end. At least I must have stayed on my feet. I can't imagine what I must have said. It could have been anything, but I guess it must have been something contentious. I waited until Molly finished her shift. She wanted to go to the Montpelier on Choumert Road. The

Montpelier was a soulless gastrotastrophe of a place, with dog treats in jars and Home Counties accents everywhere. We sat out front in the smoking area with pints. We were surrounded by the beautiful people, the *c'est magnifique*, all in their late 20s to 30s, and all of whom appeared to occupy a variety of closed club industries. They talked on and on about the housing market, stamp duty and ski holidays, drinking IPAs and cocktails. They would no doubt all go out later and writhe under neon lights in bars with video games, never once thinking about their futures that were so bright they would surely blind them. I thought about the Marchioness disaster: A party boat that sank in 1989 after colliding with a dredger. I saw both vessels drifting underneath the darkness of a bridge, the dread aggregate smashing into the side of the pleasure steamer, almost tearing it in half. The wood splintered and flew apart against the great deadweight tonnage as it ripped through the deck. In a few seconds the lights were out and the wreck was gone. A dulled mirror ball bobbed around for a moment in the muck of the Thames.

Molly was nice enough but she didn't have too much to say; she liked coin pusher machines and not a lot else. She insisted she come back to mine for some reason. I was hoping we would find Lawrence in some compromising position that would disturb her enough to leave. All fours, kitchen table – stimulating his prostate with chicken bones or something. 'Don't mind me, love' he'd say as she throws up into her hands and makes for the door. But no, no one was in. Lawrence was the one I had interacted with the most in the better half of a year that I had been here. The other bloke was some kind of Eastern European. I think he was a waiter. I didn't know his name. He was stick thin and would spend all night screaming into a headset playing war games. When you walked past his room to use the toilet it would always sound like he was engaged in some form of fantasy genocide. There was no living room in the flat but there was a sofa in the kitchen. I never understood why it was there and I had never seen any of the other freaks that lived here use it. We piled onto it.

'You're not just looking for a fuck right?'

'No,' I lied. It came out easily enough.

She was a small thing, about 5'2, and her pale skin looked sickly against the humming dead light from the fridge. We embraced into a passionless long dull drunk fuck. It was an embarrassing one, she was shrieking her head off the entire time with fake noises. She looked at me so fondly it made me feel sick. Her eyes locked onto mine and flared with infinite trust. I felt disturbed. I was an imposter and a sick bastard, leeching off her affection out of sheer boredom and loneliness. Just because I could. I didn't cum and wasn't interested if she had. I don't remember stopping. In the morning she had to open up the bar again so that was that.

6

Six months before, on the 3rd of June, a van mounted the pavement by London Bridge and mangled pedestrians before crashing into Borough High Street. Three men then ran into the market and began stabbing anyone they could around the pubs and restaurants with twelve inch kitchen knives strapped to their wrists. They killed eight people and injured nearly fifty in under ten minutes. They were shot dead and, upon inspection, found to be wearing fake explosive vests. At the time I had been working at a city boy shithole called *The Wheatsheaf* on Stony Street, right in the middle of it all. I would mostly just spend eight hours a day drifting around on benzos and collecting glasses. Almost every day a different bouncer would mistake me for a bag thief. On that evening I got home and saw the mayhem on the news. A Scottish lad called Tom had been hired at the same time as me. We didn't ever work together, but in rotation; we only saw each other when one arrived to take over from the other. It had been 50/50 which one of us would have been working that evening. Tom had survived, but was intensely claustrophobic, and when he was forced to hide from the chaos in the cellar, he came apart. Several weeks ago, I had been drinking along the Holloway Road, in an old Savoy cinema that had been gutted into a *Wetherspoons*. It was there, across the bar, that I saw Tom for the first time since the attack. His face appeared briefly behind the taps and whitened as we pretended not to recognise each other. He waited for his drink, was served, and then he left. We never said a word. What is strange to me now, which I didn't give a second thought to at the time, was that I tried to go in for my shift in the morning.

When I got to London Bridge the next day, it was all cordoned off with large yellow hoarding. The officer looked at me blankly when I told him that I needed to get to work. I went home that morning, worried only about my job. There was still a hundred quid left to find for the rent and a missed day always had consequences. The pub called me several days later to inform me that I was needed that afternoon, and not to talk to the press under any circumstances. When I came in the place looked like it had been bombed. I was surprised that nothing had actually gone off. Bullet holes decorated the exposed brick walls; gimmick art and fake hardback books littered the floor. Myself and the other more fortunate employees had to spend the afternoon cleaning up after the attack for minimum wage. That evening, two or three executives came down from the corporate office of the chain brewery and gave permission for the management to order pizza. They ended up splurging out on two Mediums for eleven people.

The slices ended up having to be cut in half. The rest of the staff were either dead or in critical conditions. One of the absent managers, Gareth, had been stabbed from one hip to the other – he was somehow alive. A nineteen year old bar girl, no taller than five foot, who only wanted to sing, was left with severe PTSD after being stabbed in the neck. After the attack, she could no longer leave her house without constant visions of Final Destination-style death scenarios. Planes would drop from the sky and decapitate her world that had once been beautiful. I sat down upon a stool and ate my half slice of pizza, before resuming my role as a terror janitor.

7

I found some work online at the London Hilton on Park Lane, lasted one shift and never went back. In doing so, I had to forfeit the £44 day's wages as new employees were meant to work long enough to pay off an initial incurred uniform debt that apparently set the company back £60. The head of the loading crew was a fat scrote called George. George had a three year ban from Millwall, which did impress me as it must have taken a real creative effort. In the 1960s, when the police had finally got around to confiscating weapons from fans, Millwall supporters began pissing on rolled up newspapers, producing a hardened cosh that could either be filled with coins and wrapped around a fist or just used as is. It came to be known as the Millwall brick and an iconic crude weapon in its own right. Broadsheet newspapers were larger and therefore made the best tool. At some point, the police caught on and became suspicious of yobs nonchalantly strolling through with copies of *The Guardian*. I called George Millwall Paul. That morning we were handling a load-in for some corporate event and had begun unloading the lorries at 6am. The shift pattern could range anywhere from two to six hours, depending on the job. This meant that you would start one job at 2am-4am, go home and do whatever, then have to be back for another job from 8am-10am. The uniform I had invested in was two sizes too big. It was 'all they had', said Millwall Paul. He would keep trying to sell the idea that they were all a great bunch of mates and that there was a big emphasis on being a 'team player'. The crew was made up of other young men of various ethnic backgrounds, who would only converse with one another in grunts and a head tilt to the general direction of where the load needed putting down. As we were pulling various huge hard cases of sound equipment from a lorry and wheeling it inside the loading bay, Millwall Paul mentioned that most of the lads he tended to hire never lasted that long. There was a flicker of genuine hurt in his statement. He just couldn't seem to figure out why.

'Who just doesn't turn up for a shift?' I feigned disgust, as we wheeled a large two man case.

'That's just bad form, you make a commitment and you stick to it.' He nodded in agreement. I knew then that I would inevitably, at some point, join the ranks of the workshy flakes that wasted his time, leaving him with no closure of civilised goodbye. I imagined the breakup.

'Don't do this,' his lip quivered. The eyes strained and grew red as he fought back the tears in front of the other lads. I was Humphrey Bogart; a stone cold heart breaker.

'You deserve someone who wants to be here. I wasn't destined for this. I'd be lying to myself if I stayed here, pushing around loads all day with you.'

His voice broke.

'Why do they always leave?'

'For what it's worth, I'm sorry.'

The case crashed against the railings of the lift. I was pulled out of this intrusive psychodrama by the real Millwall Paul.

'OI! PUT IT ON THE FUCKIN LIFT CAREFULLY.'

After we were done unloading, the crew was provided breakfast in the back of the function room of the hotel. There were two chafing dishes, piled in with the stodgy heat lamp thick white fat bacon rolls. I told them I wasn't hungry and was going out for a fag and never came back.

About fifty minutes later I was sitting in the *Joiners* trying to recruit someone to day drink with me. I was repeatedly told: 'It's 10 in the morning on a Tuesday. No I can't come for one.' Madness; eight million people were living in this city and I couldn't find one to put up with me for a couple of hours. Whatever happened to no man left behind? It dawned on me after several pints that I wouldn't be paid for that morning stint. There was no way I could afford to stay any longer. Being skint often didn't feel much like living – you just couldn't do anything. In films you always saw down-and-outs hanging around in dive bars, always with enough to drink. How did they afford that? It never made any sense to me. Life felt like a waiting room or a bus stop – just one half-arsed beautiful inconvenience after another. The first place I ever worked was at the Brighton Marina Harvester when I was 18 years old. Brighton was a place where everyone subscribed to the utopian Guardianista fantasy that it was a panacea of tolerance instead of what it actually was; just a pretentious filthy seaside town with huge social problems. There was one sickly bloke who showed me the ropes. For some reason, half of his intestines had been removed. His locker was always filled with empty and half full bottles of morphine. He worked on the salad bar. I think I was meant to eventually replace him. He may have been dying, but I can't remember – passing the torch. My sole responsibility was to replenish the salad bar with various pastas from industrial tubs that were made in the sink under a blistering tap. There were also vats of split, oily dressings and crispy onions. I would stand at the side and every ten minutes would have to slop more of it into this refrigerated trough, as the fucking pigs descended. I lost that job for using the ovens as mirrors to do my hair.

After leaving the pub I went across the road to a cafe called Eddie's. It was an American diner sort of place-cum-greasy spoon. The coffee was 90p. I sat by the door. Buses would come past every two minutes and block any light from entering the place. There were signs saying 'NO FILMING' and 'AS OF THE 24TH OF AUGUST 2015 CREDIT IS OBSOLETE'. Just who had been getting fry ups on tick, and how many they must have had before it was considered taking the piss preoccupied me for a time. Everyone else in there seemed to be either an ambulance driver, a scaffolder, or visibly mentally ill. One of the latter was at the counter chewing the ear off the owner.

'...not unless you got a wonky eye, Steve,' called across some scaffolder from a plastic chair.

'You look like the one who's cross eyed!'

'Don't cause any trouble Steve!' warned another man on a table closer to the counter. Steve was clearly retarded and was given a fair amount of leeway. My phone buzzed and displayed a voicemail. I dialled, pressed one and waited – voicemails were never good news.

A deflated voice came through. 'Good afternoon, this is George from Definitive Crew,'

'Fuck,' I said aloud and quickly hung up.

There was no way I was in the right frame of mind to find any entertainment in Millwall Paul screaming down the phone at me. I leaned back in my chair and reflected; I really did have to stop closing so many doors for myself; now I could never frequent as a guest at the Park Lane Hilton without the off chance of being bundled into a van and having ten shades of shite kicked out of me by a man deemed by Millwall as someone who takes it a bit too far.

I walked home in the midday sun, the back way so that I could see a few nice houses on Grove Park Lane. In the corner of my eye, people were living in their front rooms. Walking past the houses slowly, without turning my head, I lingered just long enough to get a subliminal flicker of their human closeness. Then, as I wandered through the St Giles' churchyard, a man in camo jogged towards me from the end of the path. Every few feet, he would stop, drop and roll, before pulling up finger guns and taking aim at the crows. A one man insurrection. I wished him well.

8

A year ago my stepmother had died of lung cancer. I had a bad toothache the day I found out she was being moved into the hospice. It turns out she hadn't just been "very sick", as my father had let on. The toothache seemed to be a bad omen of sorts, as they tended to fall out so often in my dreams. On one summer afternoon, maybe early August, on a morning I can't see myself forgetting, I was sitting on the toilet at a friend's house that I had been drinking at for several days. Chewing and tonguing every part of that yellow, hollow tooth, the surface felt like a tiny gritter lorry had made its rounds all over the enamel. I got up and spat the blood into a plugless sink before wandering back through the garden, picking the wine scum off my lips and grabbing another beer from the crate on the kitchen counter. Two friends were sitting on chairs in the foliage, smoking, whilst a third was trying to open another bottle of wine with a shoe. He had insisted that it could be done by placing the bottom of the bottle in the shoe and then banging it against the wall. He had started before I had gone into the bathroom but he was still there beating his shoe against the garden wall like dust out of a rug. After sitting for ten minutes, drinking my beer and trying to forget about the pain in my mouth, my phone rang with the news.

The garden became smaller and smaller in my vision as the tears started to roll down my cheeks. My chest felt hollow and as I looked around, the usual effortless synchronisation of reality appeared to glitch, ever so slightly. I went back through the kitchen, into the bathroom and looked down at the blood in the sink. I leaned into the mirror, opened my mouth and pushed down hard on the tooth. It shifted and collapsed into three small pieces, as it turned out that dreams could come true.

9

The Job Entry Targeted Support scheme, or JETS if you go in for acronyms, had the resources to sponsor certain claimants that weren't deemed too much of a lost cause. JETS was provided by a third party, originating from Australia, that had somehow ended up securing a contract with the Department of Work and Pensions; acting as a sort of self-described rehabilitation service for the Jobcentre. They provided what they liked to refer to as a 'Restart Scheme'. There were a variety of training programmes that were available in order to broaden an individual's employability and make them more appealing to the job market. For the most part, I had been able to play off many of my revolving redundancies as a string of bad luck, and a result of factors beyond my personal control. This place was downsizing, that one was "seasonal", compassionate leave, what have you, it went on and on. Any realities of insubordination, absenteeism or general apathy had been sidestepped. It was for this reason I believe that I had been selected for further training – compulsory, of course. This is how I ended up being booked onto a Security Guard course provided by the SIA – unabbreviated, the Security Industry Authority.

This course ran for 22.5 hours over three days at the Queen Mother Sports Centre in Pimlico, just before Victoria Station on the Vauxhall Bridge road. Attempts to legitimise the standards and practices of those entering the security industries had finally been established through this authoritative body and had been realised in 2004. Before then, fuck knows, wild west. As a prerequisite to attending in person, various online e-learning modules were expected to be completed. They mainly consisted of long videos focused on anti-terroism, with tedious interactive evacuations. The objective for the learner was to accurately locate the correct emergency exits as some exceptional set of circumstances unravelled in the building. As long as you could identify the difference between a wall and a door with a limited degree of accuracy, then you could join the module's 98% pass rate. I thought about that 2%, and the dead I'd met on London Bridge.

After the anti-terror there came the Conflict Management Unit, made up of multiple choice questions which were increasingly amusing. Without reading the questions, the answers appeared to follow a recognisable pattern of several reasonable responses and one unhinged reaction. The purpose of such tests, presumably, was to weed out the vast numbers of psychotic applicants who were drawn to such an industry where the study of a "Progression To Violence" escalation model was a core text, of which the unsurprising steps listed were: Frustration, Anger, Aggression and Violence. The final question was: What does empathy involve?

I arrived at the leisure centre at around 8am and my anxieties of being at the wrong venue were quickly dispelled when I saw three other misfits in black fleeces and trackies, hanging around outside, who were unmistakably also there to undertake the same licensing. They were men. One was smoking, and offered one to the other.

He shook his head and raised a palm. 'My body's a temple.'

'Yeah, well, mine's Chernobyl.'

I walked past them, through the automatic doors, and awkwardly shoved my way through a turnstile. The conference room was upstairs and past the swimming pool. In a windowless room with a purple lino floor, a handful of chairs and a projector, was the course instructor Darren, and about twelve other candidates. Darren did not look like a security guard but had apparently been a veteran of *Sainsbury's*. He was shoddily groomed but had made an attempt, in a white buttoned shirt, grey trousers and trainers. Projected onto an off white wall was some CCTV footage that after several minutes began to loop. It was from 3:36am in 2010. The edited footage showed a tall light skinned man in a white shirt and jeans marching down an empty high street with clear purpose. He turns a corner, and approaches another man who is drunk and attempting to slowly get home. With seemingly no provocation whatsoever, the white-shirted man then punches him square in the jaw. The drunk collapses. The white shirted man then proceeded to stamp on the drunk's head eight or nine times. It was a rapid flurry and had to be rewatched several times to get the precise count. He saunters off down the road about 20 metres before coming back to the drunk heap and bending down to talk into whatever was left of his ears. He exits, before being picked up by police a few seconds later. He goes without a fuss, and through the grainy footage seemed almost relieved. He had achieved what he set out to do and exorcised whatever was in him that night. The purpose of my watching this was so I could then demonstrate my ability to write an incident report, which is exactly what Darren had to do with this clip back in 2010. I finished my report as others on the course were arriving late and with each one the footage had to be replayed for several minutes. By ten past nine I had seen the assault maybe forty times and the scene became like a malignant dance. The whole exercise seemed rather unnecessary. There was no need for such smart-casual violence this early in the morning. Why couldn't we have just been watching someone shoplifting?

It turned out that the three old boys I'd seen out the front had been doing security for St Paul's Cathedral for the last thirty years. Recently, the management of the site had been taken on by a new firm, who insisted on making all the Cathedral's employees SIA approved. These three men had quite literally sat on their arses for decades and were now being forced to comply in the modern world of licensing infrastructure. Over the course of the day, every step for them was painful and difficult to watch. They were totally fucking useless and took several attempts to satisfy Darren in his responsibility of scraping these armchair retards past the line of basic, qualifying adequacy. In every assessment from bag searches to CPR, there was some misstep that required the procedure to be repeated. The final hurdle of the day was a "practical examination" involving a metal detector search. The day finally came to pass as the last of the three, an ungainly 68 year old Vietnamese man, completed without fault the search procedure. It was his sixth attempt and the whole room was silent. The suspect stood with arms outstretched, faithful to the incoherent instruction of the old man; he delicately stroked the wand from wrist to wrist as if performing some ceaseless commendation.

Suffice to say, I did not finish the course. One day of pulling teeth would turn out to be enough. Darren came out of the toilet as I walked past on my way back to the conference room.

'Hi,' he half mumbled. 'Good lunch?'

'Yeah, alright.'

'Nice work with the CPR by the way, that was textbook,'

'Yeah, well, only two more days then never have to do this again, huh?'

He didn't respond. There would be sick days and weekends, every now and again a holiday, but he would be doing this every day, from this piss right now until God knew when. We made our way back in silence.

10

An uneventful, solitary week went by and I was back at the Jobcentre. They had left me a message with a time and a date to attend what they called a "Commitments Review". I presumed to discuss what had happened on the security course and why I had not finished it. The appointment had originally been scheduled a few days earlier but I had been too pissed. About a half hour before I managed to scramble together a text citing "obligatory family personal religious cultural circumstances" as the reason for my unavailability. The builders were coming round and someone had to be here to let them in. There had also been a fatal shooting on my road and the police needed a witness statement. On top of that, I had jury service and then a driving lesson. I finished putting together the final touches of my insane morning with one eye open, then put down my phone before rolling over back to sleep. When I sobered up and read it the panic set in. Several days went by living in anticipation of a sanction – I would have to abandon cigarettes altogether and only drink at home. After living on increasingly limited funds for a while, there came a point where you began to start wishing time away, in waiting for a payday. This was a difficult and pathetic realisation. Each day completed without spending anything at all would be a tragic little victory. As your balance stagnates, your self esteem tends to decline with it, often without initial detection. Perhaps you could take some small pleasure in the defiance of your "opting out", but nevertheless, it did not feel like really living at all. The alternative was also detrimental to the spirit; even if you aim to do something righteous with your life. You work for a homeless charity, for instance. You get up every day, go into an office and sell your time for an objectively noble cause. But how can you claim your purpose is to eradicate this evil, that of homelessness, when the final resolution of that social trauma is against your best interests as an employee? The continuation of that trauma is a business from which you stand to gain your current way of life. This virtuous contract is a lie and one built on fear of penury and nothing more. The dentist wants your teeth to rot. Doctors hope you get cancer. The only person who wishes for your aspiration is a thief.

The payment still came through. Along with it I got the invitation to the Commitments Review. It did not sound friendly. The grace period with these people could end at any time. It was a very fragile relationship. I arrived twenty minutes early and dressed in a blue cotton button up shirt in a pathetic attempt at damage control. I was, afterall, here to showcase my brand. Hear me, another dream defeated, willing participant, ready to negotiate my wholehearted surrender to the workforce. I walked through the automatic doors and headed straight for the blue polyester sofas. After about ten minutes of sitting and rehearsing my humility, she came and sat down opposite me. The sofas were arranged about three metres away from each other. I looked over my right shoulder at Tanu at her desk, her eyes were behind glasses and glazed over underneath a headset. Then I came back to the girl. She had long wavy dishwater blonde hair that fell down her back, huge grey eyes and a freckled complexion that peppered her face. She looked like Ophelia drowning in the river. I had never particularly thought about having a type before but from now on this would be the uniform. She was just sitting there half slouched with her legs spread like a man. Her eyes were wide and aimed at the floor, as if she was sticking up a daydream. I don't know why, but I decided to talk to her as if I had known her for years.

'What are you thinking about when you do that?'

She looked up. After about four seconds of eye contact I became convinced I had somehow been walking around with shit on my face all morning and looked away.

'People only ask you what you're thinking about because they want to tell you what they're thinking about,'

'Yeah?'

'Yeah. Their lips are always moving as I tell them,' her eyes went back to holding up the floor.

I looked over again at Tanu, who was now opening up a can of Irn Bru.

'So you may as well just tell me what you're thinking about first,' she said.

'I want to drink,'

'Don't you have an appointment?'

'I just came by to tell them I found some freelance work. I was walking past and thought I'd do it in person but I could just as easily do it over the phone.' What was money anyway? It came and went.

11

Her name was Sally. She was nineteen and had initially had aspirations as a painter before she went to art school; having briefly attended St Martin's, before leaving shortly after the end of the first term. I too had dropped out of an English course the previous year. After seeing the abilities of some of the other students, she began to doubt her own talent. It did not take long for this to gather momentum, and quickly led to daily confrontations with her own mediocrity. Initially, she would be one of the first to arrive at the studio. She took pride in her early risings and self discipline. She reasoned that you needed to treat painting like a full time job, if you wanted to take it seriously. But after only a few weeks, her enthusiasm waned. She would turn up only for the compulsory criticism sessions with tutors and hardly at all for her own practice. Ultimately, she became, as not enough of us do, afflicted by a mortal crisis of self belief. This became her dread. She claimed that her reason for leaving education was to 'work it out for herself' and she would talk about this set-back with a mask of defiance, as if she always knew what she was doing, now and all along. After abandoning her painting she went into constant cycles of reinvention and phases. Her current incarnation was that of a video artist; she had only two videos to show me on her YouTube channel. One was a three minute piece of her crushing food underneath her bare feet – mainly ice lollies, raw meat and easily mushed vegetables. I asked her why she did this but she wasn't sure. She initially had thought the idea was provocative but, like with her painting, she had hit a wall with it. The video itself hadn't gotten much attention. For her second piece she had another female student go down on her underneath a desk while she painted a bowl of fruit. She showed me on her phone as we sat in *The Prince Albert* on Bellenden Road. This one, however, had been doing rather well. The view counter at the bottom read over 10,000. She was excited by its potential, but couldn't for the life of her figure out why this piece appeared to gather so much more attention than the former. I did not have the heart to tell her. Instead, I just watched as she bit her bottom lip, her face occasionally scrunching up to stifle any involuntary moans. The primary colours morphed into each other on the paper, making a smeared brown fusion of demolition orgasm. I thought of dirty protests as

I joined the ranks of the 10,000 other hard-ons all around the world.

After two hours we had a few minutes go by in relative quiet. Rain sloshed around on the tarmac outside, sirens deafened and faded away. I took a big pull on the foam of my pint.

'You know what I hate?' I began.

'You always seem to talk about things you hate,' she observed.

I recoiled. I was rumbled. Sally seemed to only talk about the things that she loved. This would likely become one of the very defining differences between us, one that would no doubt ultimately lay the groundwork for any mutually assured demise. Sensing my discomfort she changed the subject.

'So, you're writing a book? That's why you were at the Jobcentre?'

'Yes. Research. Everything I do is research. It's the only way I can justify my life to myself,'

'And how's it going?'

'Slowly.'

'What's it called?'

'Right now it's: *And Then My Broken Heart Bled Out My Arsehole*'

'You gonna put me in?'

'Why not?'

She giggled. I thought I saw her chest flush as she leant on the table and started tearing at the graphic health warning on her tobacco pouch.

12

I half woke up the next morning to the builders at work and with Sally's head on my chest and her left hand cupping my balls with sun coming through the break in the blinds. The beer had laid on the usual thick grog in my head that wouldn't clear for approximately six to nine hours. She stirred slightly and moved her hand up to my cock and rested it between her fingers like a cigarette. I started to get hard in her hands. She took my throb and started slowly rubbing it against her clit. Her eyes never opened but her lips parted slightly as she released a barely audible exhale. She kept rubbing it in circles, over and over. When I couldn't take the friction of her pubic hair anymore, I rolled over on top of her and pressed against her pussy. It held there for a few seconds before being enveloped and our pace became slow. She had mentioned the night before that she'd been bleeding for months but it had been dark and I was drunk when we first tried. Every now and then I would pull out and look down at my cock, all pulsing and bludgeoning, now resembling a crude tool in some vicious domestic slaying; I thought about fucking her to death. Then her eyes opened up and found mine and she sighed my name. I could hear the banging of hammers in the flat above, the abrasive chipping of floor tiles in the communal hallway and the endless drills. It sounded like the building was being torn apart around us and I knew then that I was also condemned and in love and there was no possible good that could ever come of it. She left an hour or so later. I offered her breakfast and a shower but she declined. She kissed me awkwardly on the cheek before ducking out of the front door, and walking down the stairs with little grace. I closed the door and went back into my room and looked out the window. I heard a quickfire succession of "NO, NO, NO, NO" from a builder, followed by a chorus of deep cackles from some others. She had hopped straight into some wet cement. She played it off with a sort of apologetic curtsey before launching into a determined power walk down the street, around the corner and presumably out of my life.

13

"It will rain this morning, again in the afternoon, and also tomorrow."

The Norwegian weather app I had recently downloaded was both remarkably reliable whilst also amusing in its English translation. Every morning, I would look up the forecast and read back its needlessly dramatic affectation, often in the weary voice of Richard Burton; such playful rituals I had come to find were essential when confronting the day. A few weeks had passed and I hadn't heard anything from Sally. I thought about her often; she didn't so much cross my mind but rather detonate it and I routinely masturbated to our last encounter, usually after looking up the weather. But as each night passed, the memory of her would fade a little more. There had been a bit of luck on my end as a friend had managed to sort me out with some landscaping work. Gardening, I thought, why the fuck not.

'...Yeah they don't need anyone skilled or anything so I thought of you,' he explained down the phone. 'Just someone to help with the labouring before the designer comes in.'

Looking down out of my bedroom window, I wondered what it would be like to have a tended garden, instead of two fly tipped cat towers and a smashed litre of vodka. These were fairly recent additions to the front bit and I doubted that they would be going anywhere soon. Someone's cat must have died. What decadent little bastard had two of them? An emperor must have fallen.

'What's the rate?'

'You got something else lined up?'

'I just like to get my invoices in order beforehand.'

He laughed at me.

'It's £100 a day, cash.'

The opportunist took me. Cash was king. Cash no one had to know about. Universal Credit wouldn't need to know.

'Yeah, alright, I got nothing on.'

A passerby below inspected the cat towers; they picked at the faux fur lining before stepping over the broken glass and continuing on their way.

In the past, when I had ceased to be on the payroll of a company, my online targeted ads began to almost immediately reflect my declining social class. Under gainful employment, I gave little thought to the more high-end supermarket adverts for premium ready meals aimed at the discerning working professional. It was only when they were replaced by relentless marketing for sperm donation and flu camp that I knew I was in a bad way. Here it was; they were after my cum and my physical well-being. No one can live completely freely, and I would not be granted something for nothing. You were always expected to pay somehow, if not from your pocket then from your fluids. The only way to really win is to be infertile, and to roll the dice for the placebo. The landscaping job was in Twickenham and fairly easy to get to; it ended up being just under an hour by bus and national rail from Vauxhall. I had had very few reasons to go out west before. Coming out of the station, I took a left down what would have been in the summer a leafy and delightful Zone 5-twat-upon-Thames suburbia. On turning the corner, an upper middle class family was doing the school run, no doubt to some independent prep school, the kind where you were assigned a personal tailor from the age of 5 or something. Two children ran ahead in their ridiculous caps and baby blue blazers, away from, who I presumed was their nanny – her demeanour was one of being on shift rather than of genuine maternal care. I hoped they got molested or their fathers would soon be set up as a patsy for some fiscal scandal and carted away from their Victorian, seven bedroom semi – away to the nick where they would have sugared kettle water thrown in their faces, or maybe just be eaten away by arse cancer. I thought about their inherited futures, and what they would grow up to be. The path was paved long ago, and there would doubtlessly be little deviation. But they hadn't really done anything to anybody just yet.

I arrived a little after 9, at a large detached house with a skip out the front, likely worth several million pounds. The only other people on the site were the Polish builders, who would always turn up early. I had been warned that they could be cold; landscapers were perceived as soft labour, flower boys with water features and M&S sushi lunches. Throughout the course of the week I mostly kept to myself and after several days of endlessly carrying bags of topsoil, never eating in front of them, and only stopping to smoke, I had earned the occasional grunted nod on the way to the portaloo. The final two days were solely for digging and I loved every hour. Exhausting yourself over the earth felt noble and rewarding. I had found something in it. The late November ground was hard and cold. I liked to destroy the soil. I felt like a free man volunteering on a chain gang. By the end of the week the pit was sixty centimetres deep and five metres squared. Recognising peaceful moments in life tends to be a harmful thing, but right now I was just a man who dug a big hole and was sitting in it – just me in this big hole that I dug.

14

We drove for about forty minutes from Wolverton, a town northwest of Milton Keynes, to the Cynthia Spencer Hospice in Northampton. It was early on a Saturday afternoon and my father had picked me up from the station. The sky was grey and through the breaks of trees it blended with the steel beams that stretched along the trunk road. Much of the relatively short drive was made in silence, until we pulled up to a zebra crossing that led to the entrance of the Centre: MK, the UK's tenth largest shopping centre.

'These cunts,' he said, gesturing to the pedestrians.

'Uh huh,' I plugged my phone into the charging port.

He shook his head. 'Fuckin zombies,'

'Innit, what can you do?'

He pulled his bottom lip into his mouth and exhaled through pursed lips. I immediately regretted the opening; I'd had every intention of killing the conversation dead.

'You see...these cunts, they don't care about anything. All they know about, and want to know about, is consumption...All they know is chain stores. Every fucking Saturday, the sleepwalkers.'

He flashed his headlights and beckoned the family to cross the road. My eyes followed them over to the car park that lay parallel to the behemoth of a shopping centre, skeletal and imposing; its black glass windows and countless stores oversaw the manic weekend trade like an impotent God of high street retail; unable to satisfy the endless march of those relentless, new-town hoarders. The car pulled away.

15

I began to receive daily missed calls from what I was fairly sure was my work coach, Tanu, trying to reach me. There was something about those final three digits (644) that triggered some abdominal dread. On my last day at the Twickenham site, in my hole, I checked my Universal Credit portal for any updates. There was a flurry of entries over the preceding weeks, the first of which was sent on the day I had met Sally. It read:

Hello,
Important Action required
You did not attend your Commitments Review at 11am on the 27th November 2017.

Your appointment has been automatically rescheduled to 9am on the 2nd December 2017.

Failure to attend your next appointment could result in your claim being closed so please take immediate action.

Regards,
Tanu

I stubbed out my cigarette in the dirt and got to my feet. These were normally fairly easy to outmanoeuvre on their own, but it was followed by a similar message, only this time with the added and emboldened:

IMPORTANT ACTION REQUIRED FINAL REMINDER.

There were a few other entries with hostile subject headings. In the half second I had checked, there were repeated flashes of URGENT and

FAILED. They really cut through, but it wasn't enough. If experience had taught me anything it was that they did have me pegged; I was, when it came down to it, a man of inaction.

16

I walked through the cold and the rain to the post office over the road, past the letterbox and opposite the wanky bakery. There were always long lines at opening time, every weekend. The image of the artisanal breadline had always been comic to me. Such queues for bread made me think of the Great Depression or subsistent relief on the Eastern Bloc, but the middle classes here appeared to love it. I deposited my wages from the landscaping and went to the cashpoint outside to check it was all there. After punching in the PIN, I looked down in disbelief, and stood there for a few moments, ignoring the tutting single pram behind me. An additional £800 was inexplicably there. Blind luck, beautiful luck – a second payment must have been made by the Department of Work and Pensions. The overall figure wasn't excessive, but the absence of a minus sign before the balance gave it a certain and welcome degree of zhuzh. Benefit fraud – I thought about it for a time. The term excited me. Fraud. He defrauded the system. He got away with it. He cheated. He fucked us all. The degenerate, the renegade. He escaped to some failed state with thousands in leeched funds and lived out the rest of his days as a full-time sex tourist. Yes, I would like to print my balance. I took my card and receipt and headed home.

Back in my room, I paced the carpet, still holding onto the balance receipt. All in all, I was now sitting on around £2100 from wages and the double UC – enough for a modest attempt at romance. After all, what were these rare instances of limited financial good fortune for, if not to take advantage of a bit of life? The fatal realisation had continued to elbow its way to the foreground, and had become increasingly hard to ignore. In a way, it had become rather like breathing. A constant function, awareness of which made you profoundly uncomfortable. Sometimes I would find myself trying to identify every imaginary abrasion. I would hold my breath for as long as possible, filling the air to see if my lung capacity had depleted since I had last been aware that I had organs. There was only one way of truly knowing and that was when they had you cut up on the slab. What was it that normal people did when they found unexpected savings – I'm sure that went on – a trip, most likely. Broadening horizons, creating memories and so forth. I looked around for my phone. There was now the briefest of opportunities for time. Time had been unforgivably wasted – a natural side effect of committing oneself totally to boredom, rather than conformity. All those days drinking, always drinking – they had stacked up – whilst trying to level over the memories, a wilting flower in a jar of piss. Any previous calls from destiny had just been pocket dials. Now there was a window for time spent in the love of another and in another place altogether – it did not matter how far away. My phone pinged, I followed the sound underneath a pillow – where dreams were culled in the mornings. There was a "gentle reminder" for the rent. That was that, I blocked my landlord's number, then found Sally's. We arranged to meet. Hi, how are you? At the Albert – the same place as before.

17

I waited out the back of the pub on the patio for around twenty minutes, spending most of this time ruminating over a mild humiliation that had just occurred at the bar. The interaction had gone as follows: I walked in the back door after noticing the usual front one was locked, and earnestly asked "You open?" to the two potential barmen/landlords, who were sitting at the bar.

'Be surprised to find out how you got in if we weren't' said one.

'Nowhere's safe anymore,' zinged the other.

Har. Har. Har.

Eventually, her head floated by a window as she went for the front door. It opened this time. She entered then went straight for the taps. After her drink was poured, she scanned the pub and clocked me outside. Wandering over with purpose, she sat down with Guinness. I already had two in front of me, one two thirds empty. It had been around three weeks. In that time I had somehow quite forgotten how much she stunned me. My mind's eye had been continuously stitching together an underwhelming manifestation. Her eyes, lips, tits and cunt were formed by a mashup of memory, pornography and imagination. The game was now to keep the true picture in front of me, for as long as I possibly could. She dipped her head and smiled warmly, looking at me with glad grey eyes. A tiny pleasurable distortion filled my head as I felt my brain turn to glass, like in the Children's skulls of Vesuvius and Hiroshima.

We sat there for a while until we ran out of tobacco and had no further purpose being out in the -1°, so opted to go through to the back of the pub, on a table in an alcove. There were just a few old boys left holding up the bar. Sally turned out to be hard to anticipate and her reactions increasingly unpredictable. The way in which she would take in information, digest it and then decide what to spit back out ran on pure gut and reflex. She would often be very matter of fact, when she could see clear resolution, but also debilitatingly indecisive. Occasionally, I would slip in lines from films into conversation to see what she would do, and she always left me with a delightfully candid response. At the same time, she could become overwhelmed by the most inconsequential of decisions. When faced with what to order, or where to go, she appeared to have a coping pattern of initial panic, followed by emotional resignation, before ultimately shutting down and disengaging. She was fond of asking questions and at some point brought up parents.

'What do you reckon your Dad would say about you if he was forced to be honest?'

'Recently he said that I was just a middle class child, off the rails with no ambition. He said he was kidding but it didn't strike me as something you would say off the cuff. So maybe that,'

'What about your mum?'

'She used to tell me as a kid that I would never get anywhere in life with a terrorist surname but I managed to get nowhere in spite of that.'

She laughed at that one and reached over for my hand, squeezing it gently in hers.

It took almost three hours but I finally felt equipped to ask her. The place had livened up slightly as the evening came; the old boys at the bar had maybe two other tables to talk across to. There were occasional jeers and dogs barking. A baby cried and was taken out by a woman lighting a fag as she opened the door with her elbow.

'I don't know what your weekend looks like, but I've got a bit of time off coming up and I was thinking of maybe going to Paris,'

'Very nice,' she said. I suddenly felt incredibly stupid. Before letting myself sit with it for too long and second guessing myself, I got it out quick.

'Would you come with me?'

She looked taken aback – definitely caught her off-guard with that one. She tensed slightly in her seat, and her eyebrows appeared to lean in as if trying to embrace, before being almost immediately pulled apart by the prudish muscles of her forehead.

'...I just thought it would be nice.'

She looked unsure but curious. She didn't say anything at first. She just let me go on. Perhaps she couldn't tell if I was serious. I hadn't really anticipated having to sell the idea. I thought it would be a cut and dry dismissal, laughed or shrugged off, but she could tell I meant it.

'I'd like to be one of those people who can go away alone, but I'm not. Y'know like going on walks by myself. I just don't understand how people do it. There's something about being in a park or by the sea or a museum without someone you know... I can't stand it. They just feel like dead scenes to me. It doesn't make me feel alive, it just reminds me that I have nobody.'

She paused for a few moments.

'Okay.' She said. I thought I'd hit her with some Drugstore Cowboy.

'What would you say if I told you that I can't stand everyday life – like tying my shoes?

She picked up the empty glasses and stood up to go to the bar.

'Well... I'd tell you to get Velcro then.'

PA

RT

TWO

18

Two days later and it was time to go. I had made fairly decent time in arriving at Vauxhall about ten minutes before Sally, at around 9:30 am. It did not feel like I was waiting long before she stepped off the 436 bus, wheeling a modest hard shell suitcase. I had with me a black rucksack containing two changes of clothes and minimal toiletries. She looked excited; we smiled and kissed before entering the station. The Victoria line would always scream. I always thought that it sounded rather like the Luftwaffe. The Nazis had added that noise on purpose just to scare civilians shitless and I was convinced that TfL did the same. Every day, without fail, the tracks would parody the drone of dive bombing; to earth; denying commuters any mental refuge from the decisions they had made; the ones that put them on this train so very early, in what could have otherwise been such a gentle morning. For us, however, it was quite the opposite. Removed from the hateful commute, we had ducked out of that big hurry. With the green light from Sally, I went ahead and made all the necessary travel arrangements. I had booked online two nights at a hotel for 86 euros, along with Channel tickets from St Pancras to Gare du Nord. The trip would go over my birthday but I hadn't mentioned it. I was turning twenty-two.

Sally had zoned out on an advert for vitamins that was plastered above the head of a bald passenger sitting opposite. After about eight minutes we grinded through Warren Street. Everyone else was looking down, naturally.

'Can you speak any French?' she asked, without looking at me.

'No, you?' She thought for a moment and brought her eyes over.

'I can say Hello, Goodbye, and Thank You,'

'That really is fuck all,'

'Yeah well... What else do we really need to say to one another, when it comes down to it?'

She made a good point. It then dawned on me that I wouldn't be able to understand anyone in Paris, and in doing so, a new appealing dimension to the trip was opened up for me. London, for the most part, tended to be occupied by people I despised; and I was forced to understand every single word they all said. Here, though, it would be like the volume was turned down, and there were no subtitles. No one could contaminate it; we could simply be together. I looked at the pair of us sitting side by side in the dark reflections of the tube carriage.

The tunnel between Kings Cross and St Pancras International is deceptively long. Arrivals can be misleading. Sally went to use the toilet, so I wandered about the hall, just outside of the departures for the Eurostar. She was a little on edge: when coming through the barriers at Kings Cross, she pointed out a man on his knees with a laptop open on a hard case with wires and various gadgets. She asked me if I thought he was some sort of bomb disposal officer. I reassured her that I couldn't imagine they would wear flat caps. The departure gate wasn't particularly crowded. There were no frantic hurries or late travellers, everyone appeared to just float. The sound of a fastidious piano started to fill the gate, played surely by some autistic child prodigy – I tried to get away from it by ducking into a WH Smith.

The Eurostar descends to around a hundred metres below sea level at its deepest point. At this depth, the pressure increases approximately one atmospheric unit for every ten metres. When applied to the body, the results are grotesque. The lungs collapse immediately, contracting to about one tenth of their original size. The gastrointestinal tract is swiftly crushed; any air left in the sinus cavities causes rupture, as blood and fluids are spread into spaces where air has been compressed. Tissues of all sorts dissolve in a flood of nitrogen. The immediacy of this death cannot be understated or indeed taken for granted. They had tested this, I was sure; dead pigs imploding in dive suits filled my head. I considered a €2.60 can of Coke from the onboard menu. The display screen infographic that descended from the roof briefed us that the cafe was located in coaches eight and nine; we were in eleven. Other than that, there was no instruction as to which way the train numerically descended. Making up my mind, I refused to look even mildly foolish, and opted to stay in my seat, hungry and irritated rather than potentially going the wrong way. Eventually, I also needed a piss, but decided to sit with it for a good half hour before finally determining the discomfort as the cause of all my internal pain.

'I need a piss,' I announced, and unfolded awkwardly into the aisle, making my way towards the end of the coach. Walking back to my seat after relief, I checked up on the other passengers sitting in our immediate vicinity. There were two couples, one parallel and one in front, both heterosexual. The girl from the parallels had just opened up some container that filled the carriage with a sickly, offensive smell that became inoffensive once I realised that it was soup. The parallel boy started dipping Pringles in it. The couple in front appeared less enamoured, to the extent of completely ignoring each other. She was playing some indiscernible, loudly coloured phone game, her fingers swiped relentlessly across the screen. He was occupying himself with what looked like some form of travel Scrabble, shuffling the cards lethargically. I grimaced as I couldn't help but wonder how they fucked.

There are several tunnels on the way to Folkestone that all differ in duration, so you are never quite sure which one is the Channel Tunnel itself. At only 50 km long, and with the train traveling around 300 km per hour, it takes around thirty-five minutes. With each exit breached, we would try to determine if we had actually arrived. We looked at the trees, at the pylons and the hills and began to make an amusing game of it. It didn't last long, as the joy was ultimately killed by a text from my mobile phone provider warning me of the dire financial perils of roaming data charges, now that I was in FRANCE. We sat back and went into ourselves. Every so often, a sort of chiming sound would come on over the intercom, but an announcement never followed. Its alert and purpose were never revealed and remained an almost totally insignificant mystery for the rest of the journey.

We excited the Gare du Nord. Men waved illicit boxes of cigarettes for sale by the doors, others attempted to wrangle straggling visitors into taxis. We stood outside, and after a disorientating back and forth over directions – as both our phones refused to play the game – we had a general direction. Almost immediately, the dread began to slip in and I looked around for any bad omens that could confirm my suspicions that the whole thing had been a terrible idea. There was nothing unusual about the scene at all. It really was just all down to me. At the first hurdle, I was giving too much of myself away. Sally was calm and mostly unphased. We headed west, on Rue de Dunkerque, and walked down before taking a slight left onto Rue de Saint-Quentin, then left on de Magenta, right onto Rue du Faubourg Saint-Denis and then keeping pretty much true until the Hotel. It was meant to take twenty-five minutes but ended up taking the better part of an hour. One of the wheels on Sally's suitcase had at some point broken off. I took it from her and dragged it the rest of the way. There was something about lugging around a suitcase on half its wheels that made you feel like a total cunt. Approaching every curb and cobbled street I braced for embarrassment. Coming onto Boulevard de Bonne Nouvelle, the one good wheel hit some gravel and a loud rapid fire noise drew the attention of every pedestrian. With no stabilised momentum, it would veer off course whenever I tried to put it in a new direction. It would frequently fall on its narrow side and scrape across the road, demanding to be awkwardly put right again. I felt like a sitting duck, a paranoid, fumbling easy target. No one wants to look like a tourist.

The Agadir bar and Hotel Du Globe was at 197, and cosied next to Club 199 – presumably a titty bar, with its two poles flanking its large red door. The Agadir bar and hotel was a grubby thin white building, only three metres wide. On the right side was a tiny door, with the rest of the front being two large glass sliders. Plastic patio furniture was set out around two small tables that protruded halfway out onto the narrow pavement; so much so that the pedestrians either brushed past, draping their handbags over patrons' shoulders, or they took their chances in the road. The reception was a slither of a bar, where only one man could operate. An old mahogany beam stretched across the ceiling. They only had German beer, white spirits and fruit slices in jars. After a language barrier and payment standoff at check in, we were given the keys to the room. I addressed an old Arab man with a horseshoe moustache, his legs set akimbo, and propped up by the bar on his thin forearms.

'Hi, I made a booking online.' I could have probably made some effort in French, but after looking like such a tit on the walk over, I opted to appear ignorant.

'Ehh?'

We did this three or four more times before a younger man came through the back and awkwardly side-slid into the nook-bar to mediate. Once our reason for being in a hotel was understood, the older man pushed a card machine at me.

'No, I already paid through the website.' I told him, but he wasn't having any of it. Just to get settled, and because I lacked the language skills or stamina to argue any further, I paid potentially for the second time and we took the keys. From the bar, we walked through to the back of the building and climbed several flights of bulging pink stone stairs to the third floor. Uneven steps were a common feature amongst mediaeval castles, with varied heights so that invaders would trip and hopefully break something. It appeared that the Agadir had been fortified in a similar fashion. I looked up at the ceiling for any murder holes and if the old Arab was waiting at the top to pour quicklime in my eyes.

We were in room 29. The walls were also pink and bulged, but the floor tiled. There was a double futon with red bedding. The sink was next to the bed and a few feet to the right was a bidet. Right in front of the bidet were two red polystyrene swivel chairs with office-star legs that looked out through a large window sectioned into six panes. Sally placed her suitcase at the end of the bed and wandered over to the sink. She turned both taps but they would only groan. I went looking for the communal toilet that I was told was down the corridor. I found a saloon door that led to a small room with a hole in the ground. The pipes were so old that they couldn't handle anything more than a modest shit going down them. There were laminated diagrams detailing that under no circumstances would toilet paper flush down. Instead it had to be discarded in a small pedal bin.

I came back into the room to find Sally lying on her back on the bed. I wondered if she had been expecting a pair of towelling dressing gowns, folded before pillow chocolates on high thread count linens. She didn't know that the room was forty quid a night.

'The plugs don't work' She giggled.
'Come on, let's go get a drink.'

19

We went back the way we came, as this was the only way that we knew. One of the first sights to catch my eye were the large number of prostitutes hanging around, almost every twenty metres. I had not been aware of the area's notoriety as such a soliciting district when initially making the booking. They were all old, haggard and looked duck taped together. Their hair did not appear to move in the breeze, and they wore fur coats with drastic heels on their knee-high latex boots. Every time we passed, they would glare at Sally. Other than her trainers, she was not in fact dressed too dissimilar, in her denim Afghan coat. But she was young and her lips were filled with blood instead of acid. Just who was this new young cunt stealing their potential tricks? I was wearing a long leather trench coat; smiling at her, I wondered if I could pass for her pimp. The streets seemed to repeat themselves. Every road that we went down appeared to just be made up of pharmacies, opticians and fast-food outlets. Seemingly in that order, on rotation; at one point there was a gym above a McDonald's. These must have been the biggest markets: the afflicted, the inhibited, the hopeful gorgers and the vain. Back near the Gare du Nord, we found a railroad bar nearby, Le Cristal Bar, on Rue Louis Blanc.

'Deux, big ones!' Sally gestured with both hands, demonstrating the size of a pint glass to the girl behind the bar.

'Better you than me, I don't want to say a word to these people.'

We found a table out front and sat down with the beers.

'Sally you know what's funny? I began. 'I can't get anyone to sit next to me on the train. Even when it's crowded. I pick my bag up off the empty seat but still nothing. They always seem like they'd rather stand. Do I have something written on my face? Do I give off something bad?'

'Definitely,'

'Oh right.'

'People always sit by me, even on an empty carriage. I have an approachable face.'

'It's not approachable, it's magnetic,' After several pints I wanted to flip the script and mix up the order.

'I'll have a Jameson and soda this time.'

'D'you not have it with ginger ale?'

'I did until an Irishman called it a Souper'

'A Souper?'

'Yeah see, Prods would go around to starving Catholics and offer them soup if they converted.

If you took the soup you were a Souper. I felt like I had been betraying my roots. I'd been drinking the soup for years.'

She sat back for a moment. Taking the straw I had abandoned by my drink and placing it in her own, she covered the end with her finger and pulled it up, before letting the rum and Coke fall back into her glass.

'Are we yuppies?' she asked.

'You are, I'm just on the sideline.'

'But you're here with me?'

'Yeah but, you've got the postcode'.

'..So what do you have going on when we get back?' she asked

'To tell you the truth, not a whole lot.'

'Well what are you gonna do?'

'Does it matter?'

'Not really, but you have to do something,'

'Maybe I'll just stay here and become a sex trafficker.'

She smiled and then pursed her lips, swaying her head from side to side as if weighing up the pros and cons.

'...Flexible hours.'

We walked hand in hand most of the way with only a rough idea of the line to take back to the hotel. The streets were quiet. With the glow of booze and Sally's warmth by my side, I began to feel as though I had really cheated something. We said very little. Occasionally, she would hop and skip and I would kick at some litter. Back at the Hotel du Globe, we staggered up the stairs, laughing and tripping over each other. We fell on our bed in the dark. Our lips met slowly, and continued to slow. I told her that I loved her. Her eyes were almost closed when her grin grew wide and her freckles combined in harmony as she told me that she loved me too. She fell asleep a few moments later and I gently pulled my arm out from underneath her. I lay back on the bed. The ceiling was pink, splotted and bulging.

20

The next morning my phone pulsed me awake. The message read:

Hello,
Important Action required
You did not attend your Commitments Review at 9am on the 2nd of December 2017.
Please be sure to report a change in circumstances. Failure to do so will result in your claim being closed. As a result of your absence from your Commitments Review, your next claim WILL be sanctioned.
Regards Tanu
I had indeed failed to report a change in my circumstances to the Department of Work and

Pensions. Sally's head was resting on my chest and I could feel her breathing gently. She groaned, let out a stretch and rolled over to face the wall. I stroked a finger down her side from her shoulder to her arse before bringing my fingers together and tracing her pussy. She stirred and rotated her hips before slightly parting her thighs. Arching her back, she began to move herself down onto my fingers; I held them firm as they slowly eased inside her.

Benefit expenditure had been overpaid by about 2% previously in 2016 and was estimated to rise at a non-statistically-significant rate to 2.2% in 2017. This figure was, however, the joint highest recorded rate, a level not seen since 2009. It amounted to 3.8 billion pounds. Comparably, it was estimated by Her Majesty's Revenue and Customs that there was a 33 billion pound tax gap in that year – a drop in the ocean. Regardless, I couldn't give a fuck. Sally leaned up on the bed, shuffled awkwardly to her feet with her legs together and then bounded across the room in long strides, trying not to drip any of my cum onto the floor. She sat on the bidet, wiped herself with the pink tissue paper and threw it into the bin before zoning out on the wall, as she often did.

'We ought to get a jump on the day,' she began. 'Was there anything you wanted to see in particular?'

I didn't feel well.

'Not really,'

'Well why did you wanna come here then?'

I leaned across the bed and rummaged around in my jacket and trouser pockets in the heap on the floor, looking for some Xanax. I had gotten used to keeping them on hand for particularly detrimental hangovers; ensuring they were on my person at all times would give me the same psychological comfort I imagined cyanide capsules did for those facing the unsightly – I didn't particularly regard it as a drug habit. Nevertheless, I must have left them behind, and the dread came with full force.

'I just thought it would be nice.' She seemed confused but then shrugged.

'Let's just try and make as many big stops as we can, then,' she said, raising to her feet. I took a breath and held it, looked at the floor, then the door, then the plugs, and finally at her. She went over to the sink to wash her hands.

21

I did generally try to avoid drinking when I was hungover – it really was cheating when it came down to it. That wasn't what I had a problem with, rather that once I initially started it was a real concerted effort to stop. As soon as I had that first drink, tomorrow did not exist, and right now would do just fine. From what I had observed,

Sally appeared to drink like a normal person, and it was too early for her to make a comment on my habits just yet. Often, in relationships, people tend to give you the benefit of the doubt for a while, before your inner bastard starts to show. Then it's just a matter of time to see how long they'll put up with it. This can vary greatly, but it is usually a significant amount of time. It would take a lot of foresight and self discipline to shut down chemistry and love at the first sign of trouble, regardless of its impact. It was unusual to hear about and seemed fairly inhuman to me.

It was still my birthday, but I didn't say anything. We had been walking the streets for about an hour before settling on a place to eat. I was fairly naive in regards to restaurants and it seemed like a roulette between stumbling across a charming kept secret and an underwhelming shithole. The place we ended up appeared alright at first; it had an immediately forgettable name. As a keen waiter advanced with a little too much enthusiasm, appearing almost pathetically grateful to seat us, I began to fret; consequently knocking some cutlery to the floor as I sat down. Then we opened the menus to pictures of the food and I cringed at the misstep. I watched her eyes dart around the room, giving it a once over. She had mentioned that she had had a boyfriend a year before who was violent. It had come to a head when the police got involved and that was that. She didn't tell me much else, only that she had grown a nervous disposition ever since. She seemed to me, overall, to be a deeply lonely person. You could be mistaken as dismissing her as impressionable, and simply putting her trust in the wrong people, but there are some who find comfort in being mistreated, as it's what they have been used to their whole lives. When pain becomes so familiar, its absence tends to be replaced by fear and confusion. Love and compassion are unknown and therefore were to be approached with suspicion and doubt. Adept abusers have an instinct for recognising this and will always home in on a damaged soul. Then it all tends to happen more or less the same, over and over again in a congruent harmony of perversion. I tried to hide my involuntary grimace, as intrusive flickers of her past flooded my head. Just why was it that we tended to suffer more in our imagination than in reality? A few more couples and friends were seated as sounds of laughter and pulled chairs filled the dining room. Unintelligible greetings and stories hummed all around as we smiled at each other over the ridiculous menus; here we were, two clearly broken people, trying their best to make a go of it. The waiter came over and reacquainted himself before pointing to a TV screen above the bar.

'Ahh, Johnny Hallyday?' He stared into my eyes. Johnny Hallyday was the reputed French Elvis, and had just died – it was all the country appeared to be talking about. I shrugged and said something like, 'I don't think so?'

He was appalled that I was not aware of the man who brought rock 'n' roll to France. He took our order, was further repulsed by Sally's vegetarianism, and went on his way.

'I hadn't heard of him either,' she said when he was out of earshot. We sat for a short time in silence.

'Would you fuck me if I was underage?' Sally asked, audibly. I sniggered, caught off guard and incredibly charmed. I looked around and no one cared, I remembered we were in France. Playing up to the bit, I pretended to be deep in contemplation at the moral qualm.

'Hmm, No, no I don't think I would.'

She nodded, then looked at the condiments, her mouth pursed into a wry grin. '...And WHY not?!'

We left after having a below average meal. I was drunk, she was not – I had caved. There was something about being trapped in the social dance of the restaurant experience with a hangover and a language barrier that ended up being just too much to handle unaided. She looked at me with slight unease. Sally had put together a loose itinerary at some point earlier in the morning and we began shuffling along from the restaurant to the first heading. The day-drunk was breaking in my head and nothing appeared or felt particularly real at all; I knew Sally could sense my turn as she too had fallen mostly silent.

Paris syndrome was a fascinating psychological condition. It was mostly reported by Japanese tourists, as the sense of culture shock was purportedly more extreme for those visiting from the far East. I had initially thought of the condition as just a term for a flailing, heat-death of romanticism – as the deluded individual was met with the reality that Paris was in fact just a city with crime, pollution and social problems, just as any other. What was remarkable in the cases of the Japanese tourists was the extent to which the symptoms manifested in bizarre psychosomatic displays. People reported dizziness, vomiting, derealisation and delusional states; all fairly dramatic responses to that which can be considered just a case of extreme disappointment. I pictured long queues of tourists drifting past the Louvre, sombrely marching hand in hand, over the bank and into the Seine. Others sat for caricaturists, who, on finishing their portrait, performed a consensual coup de grâce. Crowds gathered atop that great puddle iron tower in an endless ritual procession of self-disembowelment.

22

As things stood, I did not believe Paris syndrome to be the explanation for any mental phenomena I was experiencing. On that front, I just really wasn't sure. Sally asked if I was okay several times; I told her I was and that we should crack on. Amongst her list of stops were all the usual conventional museums and monuments that you would imagine for someone's first trip to a global city. I looked over at the list on her phone. She had assembled an excessive amount of sightseeing to attempt in the given time frame. The thought of traipsing through them all made me want to cry. Quite honestly, I would have rather shit in my hands and clapped. The first stop was the Centre Pompidou. The journey from the restaurant was fairly arduous, involving more than one train in the wrong direction, I managed to keep myself together and remained mostly silent – there was a chance, any time I opened my mouth, that I ran the risk of something completely hateful coming out. After a while, I had to say something and so asked her what she wanted to see. It turned out there wasn't anything on that particularly "grabbed her", but she had assured me that the building itself was worth going for as an architectural "must-see" in its own right. Initially I had been wholly dismissive of the place and on arrival I was unimpressed to the point of barely concealable agitation. My hangover, unsupervised by benzodiazepines, was progressing into a total fucking bastard. It was not possible for anyone to feel any curiosity in this state, and right now the beloved contemporary gallery might as well have been a multistory car park draped in scaffolding. Next was the Louvre, where nothing happened worthy of note; then to Notre Dame where a young Asian couple were getting married outside. She posed in her white dress with her new husband for a photographer, no doubt freezing her tits off. Between the shots she would do little hops on each foot, arms down by her sides, palms flat and fingers extended, vibrating like a hummingbird and mouthing unmistakably whatever her language was for "fuck, fuck, fuck, fuck".

23

My father had told me to "expect everything", and that it didn't matter if I laughed or cried. It can be a bit much, he said, and it tends to hit you all at once, in strange ways. I didn't take much notice. The Cynthia Spencer Hospice itself was relatively pleasant; a secluded compound of several cream brick bungalows, adorned with modest shrubbery; oak and ash trees, stood rooted in short grassy banks around the car park. The sanitiser dispenser smelt of raw alcohol and the reception was painted a bright, pacifying yellow. It looked like an A&E department, only without the typical sense of urgency – I suppose there really wasn't any. We took the first corridor on the left into a wing, it was short and her room was the first on the right. I entered and softly got out a 'Hey'. My father went over and kissed her on the forehead. She was swollen and initially unrecognisable. She had undergone a treatment of various steroids to fight the aggressive tumours that were blowing out of her brains and into her scalp. I had not seen her for some months, and she had deteriorated more than my father could seemingly bear to let on. She was mostly confused and sedated, better than anything I had known, or at least would know until whatever form inevitably took me. I felt okay, and stood over by the flowers that sat on a small end table by the window. The radio was on – a classical station – the room felt calm; my father approached her and tucked her in like a younger sibling. I couldn't hear why but he had to remind her of how the nurses had to cut off her wedding ring because of the swelling. As I looked at her fat bare fingers my heart burst and I came apart. Tears streamed down my face and a rising panic filled my chest, but I didn't want to leave. I was engrossed to watch someone face their romantic love dying, as it gave way to platonic disorder, right before his eyes, and to carry on. He reversed almost the whole way out of the car park with the gravel crackling under the cold tires.

24

Later on in the afternoon, after a forty-five minute queue, I had started to sober up as we went up the Eiffel Tower. Sally looked tired and reserved. Any enthusiasm she had had earlier in the day had all but disappeared. The hours of anhedonic sightseeing had clearly taken their toll on her spirit, to the point where she could barely conceal her indifference to the activity at hand. There it was, undeniable and written all over her face – I had corrupted her. It angered me, and the self loathing at the realisation provoked an unexpected reevaluation of my circumstances. As the lift rose, somehow, my spirits did with it. I became acutely aware that I was somewhere else and with someone special. It was unmistakable, and could only be described as a renewed sense of wonder. It crept over me in a wash of relief, as I felt myself capable of having a good time. I had to mark the moment to Sally, who was looking down at the ground below, resigned and with barely any acknowledgement.

I squeezed her hand, 'You know before I met you I would sit and have conversations in my head…'

She looked up at me.

'…You feel like an imaginary friend, come to life. I'll hold onto you like a balloon.'

She beamed from ear to ear, her cheeks filled with blood and her pupils dilated, as she threw herself around me. Then the lift stopped abruptly. It was explained to us by an apathetic steward that the increasingly poor weather conditions would prevent our group from accessing the top; consequently, we would be limited to only accessing the second platform. The doors opened, we were presented with the elements battering the landing. As fellow tourists piled out of the lift, the initial wave that ventured more than a couple of metres out from the protection of the structure began having extreme difficulty in standing upright, and many gave up and retreated, abandoning any attempts at walking to the edge to take photos. My phone buzzed and Sally went on ahead. A text message from Universal Credit informed me that they had been made aware of their error, and had opened up a case with my bank to rescind any overpayment. Moving forward, my claim was also to be terminated due to a failure to uphold the commitments of my job search. I lingered for a moment before walking out into the rain. The sky hung low, grey and mostly unremarkable. Sally was the only one out on the platform. She was running laps around the tower in the downpour, screaming, drenched, laughing and smiling.

25

I left her in a nice cafe not long after. It was a trendy place, all white except for a bruised navy wall facing the street, filled by a window that was sectioned off into horizontal rectangles; the view was one of large beige tenement blocks. The seating of minimal patio furniture was also white. It looked like an art gallery, or some other *modern liminal space*. There were no other customers. Sally had wanted to find a place to dry off. She sat down at one of the tables by the window. I told her I was just going to the toilet. To the right of the service counter there was a descending corridor to the bathrooms. Next to the women's there was a fire exit.

26

It is rare, but not unheard of, for unexploded bombs from the Second World War to be discovered laying, quite active, near the tracks of *Gare du Nord*,

Europe's busiest train station. Naturally, they cause major disruptions, as services are cancelled for an extended period of defusal. I took the bus back most of the way towards the station. There, inside a Mexican restaurant, perched at the makeshift bar of an indoor Taqueria van, I sucked on an absurdly large margarita and tried to think about what I had done. It was an extravagant drink, garnished psychotically with umbrellas, cucumber ribbons, limes, twists, jalapeno slices and edible hibiscus. I watched the slush as it made its amusing journey through the vibrant double-looped novelty straw, all its needless way into my mouth, and waited. There was no denying that the trip had been a grave and fatal error. I thought about Sally, back at the cafe; wondering how long she would have waited before giving up and leaving. What on earth did she think was happening? I just felt numb. No external sights or experiences seemed to reach me. I tried to think of the good times, and why this wasn't one. The past was always beautiful but dead, no matter what was happening at the time, and so was a source of great comfort, relief and pain. Tomorrow just didn't exist, and there was never anything worse than right now. The restaurant began to fill. The atmosphere could be recognised as festive. I left after three more.

The streets were busy for winter as I walked northeast along Rue La Fayette and after twenty minutes I came across the Le Conservatoire bar next to the Jaurès metro station. Taking over the corner, it seemed to be a vibrant spot, with a red canopy over the front tables, large windows and the typical charm of what one would expect from a Paris brasserie. I went inside and ordered Stella then sat down in the window. At first it put me on edge when the bars in Paris would not accept payment right away. It was alien to me, and seemed like blind faith. I didn't feel watched every time I left the bar for a fag, but they must have been – surely. The dim lights flickered continuously but disturbed no one. Everyone carried on as normal, normal young people with their normal young friends. I attempted to eavesdrop but couldn't understand a word, and wondered what they all said – I assumed normal young things. Reggae music played. It appeared to be roughly fifty-fifty beer and coffee drinkers. Nothing made any sense. After about an hour and a half the waiter came over and tried to ask me something. He realised I was English and then held a finger to his lip. The rest of the discourse then had to be performed through mime. I was occupying two tables and he wanted to seat a couple. It did not take long for the whole request to fall into place. I got up as he moved the tables apart to accommodate. They squeezed past me with the most polite 'merci' and sat down, now in the window. I sat back in my half table, only separated by about two feet. They were beyond a charming pair. He was bashful and handsome and dipped his shoulders as he spoke to her. She was also unsurprisingly beautiful, with her hands resting in parted thighs, leaning far over the table as she listened intently. Ten minutes went by before they would leave and I couldn't help but feel responsible. Their body language had become self conscious as I drank and stared. They had stopped stroking hands and fidgeted awkwardly in their seats. To be young and beautiful was always undermined by fear. The waiter gestured 'Another?' from across the room, I closed one eye in a slowly rung out wink, and gave back my thumb. He then appeared to hesitate, before shouting to the barman, who looked at me and signalled back six. It was likely that I would have to move on soon. The couple got up, shuffled past towards the door and left. It was 6pm.

I decided to leave the bar while it was still my decision. Often, in such sombre and needlessly defiant moods I would stay until I was asked to leave or, better still, physically ejected from the place, but I didn't appear to have it in me anymore. I made my way over to Rue St Denis and hung around. The temperature had dropped to a degree below zero, and at night it became a wholly pedestrianised zone. There were two whores that I had seen standing there the day before, occupying a doorway, and who hadn't moved much for twenty minutes. The one I made contact with for no other reason than that she was closer to me, was called Marguerite. Our exchange was polite, cordial and surprisingly enthusiastic, after which Marguerite and I headed upstairs, inside the innocuous building that she had been marketing herself in front of. She was East Asian, claimed to be twenty-five and wore a green, glittered, low cut top with high, orange latex boots. She spoke English just fine, which disappointed me greatly – I did not much feel like being understood. On a queen size bed in a plain room with red velvet curtains and a plastic mattress protector, she sat down and listed off her services and their corresponding prices. I just stood there. There was the opening massage that graduated to a variety of stress release practices, within reason, including handjobs, blowjobs, footjobs and a quickie. For twenty extra euros she also offered anal penetration, domination, striptease and roleplay. I walked over to the bed and nodded along, as if contemplating my options. Gauging my lack of enthusiasm, she asked if I wanted the Girlfriend Experience. A loud crash came from the room next door along with the sound of a man presumably ejaculating. I felt like I wanted to cry. She had made the point several times that it was a matter of strict professional standards to not do anything without a condom, and made absolutely no exceptions. I agreed wholeheartedly and with a raised hand, as if I was in court, assured her that I would not have it any other way; that it would indeed be no problem, but I already knew what was going to happen. I had surely been dead below the waist for the best part of two hours by now. She knelt down and unceremoniously pulled out my bloodless, deflated prick and began trying to wrangle its wormy form into the base of the rubber. As I swayed gently back and forth, I tried to place a hand delicately on her head, but missed, and it fell limp to her shoulder. After thirty seconds of giving her no purchase whatsoever, she held the opening of the condom firmly over my cock, squashing it flat against my groin. Now she had it on the ropes, she began licking the cling-filmed tip, like a mechanical puppy; gazing up in manic encouragement, as she attempted to kiss any life into the sad scene. She stopped after a couple of minutes, and I sank down onto the crackle of plastic.

'I'm sorry,'

'Don't be,' she said.

'I don't know what happened,'

'You don't?'

'Do you know what Paris syndrome is?'

'No.'

I pulled up my trousers, and began trying to tie my belt. 'It's a mental phenomena where visitors experience an extreme sort of culture shock that can manifest in bizarre physical symptoms, despite being psychological.'

'Uh huh.' She wandered over to a pedal bin by the small window, stepped on the lever, and discarded the partially unravelled, delipidated condom. A butterfly's life cycle can be halted as a larva, prematurely interrupted by disease.

'I wonder if that's what's happened here...'

'You drink too much,'

'It's reported mostly amongst Japanese tourists. Did you ever have anything like that coming over here?'

'I'm from Korea.'

She told me if I wasn't going to cum then I had to leave. I paid her and went on my way. The Hotel du Globe wasn't far, just a bit further down the street.

27

When I got to the hotel there didn't appear to be anyone behind the Agadir bar. I didn't have any phone data so, as I returned into the range of the Wi-Fi, the messages from Sally came through in a brief but relentless onslaught of pings. At first there was just a succession of one, two then three, but by the fourth the notifications blurred into a deranged lagging tone. I walked up the steps to our room and opened the door. Sally was laying on her back with her head on a pillow at the foot of the bed, nearest to the door. I turned the light off as her eyes looked up at me, kicked off my boots and laid down next to her. She didn't move at all, and neither did I. We lay there for a few minutes without saying a word.

'I just don't think I'll ever understand you,' she said, finally. I felt almost nothing in the dark. I closed my eyes, my own Earth tilting on its axis, and tried to surmise a profound explanation.

'It just all feels like washing up forever. Everyday is in a supermarket. I can't make heads or tails of it.' I couldn't tell if she was crying or not. I listened hard for any deviation in her breathing.

'I'm going home early tomorrow and I don't want you to come with me.'

She turned over away from me. My head felt completely blank. We fell asleep in silence.

28

In the morning, Sally had already packed her bag and cleaned up around the hotel room before I had gotten up. Any organic remnants of our stay had been completely wiped. Right before my eyes, tidied neatly away into a memory, the attempt at a weekend away was now over. Sally had wanted to visit the Père Lachaise Cemetery, the largest in Paris at 110 acres and over a million interments, some of whom were particularly influential. We were supposed to go the day before but the weather had taken a turn. Today was Sunday. I asked if I could come with her; she shrugged and said, 'If you like.'

We walked for five minutes to the Réaumur–Sébastopol métro station, on the border between the 2nd and 3rd Arrondissements, to catch Line 3 down to Gambetta, and from there it would only take a few minutes to walk to the cemetery. She had brought her luggage with her. When we got onto the train, she sat opposite me on the subway bench, which I had not expected. I thought for sure she would sit a couple rows ahead, keeping me at a sex pest's distance, forcing me to feel the shame of following a vexed woman around, several metres behind. On the map of the subway line, a light flickered over the next stop for Arts et Métiers, and after seven minutes we had arrived at ours. Coming out of Gambetta station, the closest exit for Père Lachaise takes you up an escalator that leads out directly into the street of the 20th Arrondissement. Sally stood a couple steps ahead, her hair tied up and arms folded in a chartreuse wool jacket. As we emerged onto the street level, an old man in mismatched black trainers looked at Sally, then at me as we walked past, and dipped his head in approval. We followed Avenue du Père Lachaise to 7 Rue des Rondeaux to enter the cemetery through the Porta Gambetta entrance. Up the cobblestone path, at the bottom of the hill, there is an elaborate map of the tombs and headstones. There were endless divisions, ninety or so, that didn't appear to follow any linear coherence, in addition to various lanes and avenues. I could not make any fucking sense of it. Sally hovered for a few moments before moving on, and so couldn't have been wanting to visit anyone in particular. I gave up, with her still just about in sight, and followed up the hill. In the 41st division, amongst the tightly packed allotments of grand sepulchral chapels, I came across the enclosed tomb of Mathieu. Luminous and cerulean stained glass crucifixes flanked its walls. I felt some pull and went inside. Above an altar of dead leaves and a broken stone cross, raised on the back wall was presumably Mathieu, in Victorian clothes, a left hand in his trouser pocket, in a misguided attempt at immortality in glass. When I stepped back out, Sally was gone. I continued down, occasionally staggering on the uneven cobbles. The paths were winding, overgrown and compacted by garish overlapping tombs. Imposing headstone busts of important men, now piss-soaked and weeping emerald from acid rain, stood feeble in a zoo of decay alongside stone angels, now eroding into crumbling monsters. My mouth was dry and my head felt excavated. Faintly from the other side of the path came the sound of distant, blaring techno. I walked through the bushes and followed the noise. Spat out at the back of some mausoleums, wedged in a thin gap, I held onto the stone and waded through the mud and leaves, browsing the aisles in a supermarket of bones. Once free, I was back on some other identical path, at the periphery of the cemetery, the techno pounding over the traffic. I darted back up the hill, towards the centre of the grounds. Finally, amongst some shrubbery, it was calm. I heard chattering voices around the corner. I came through the bush and saw Sally and a visibly American family standing at a metal fence that was cordoning off some of the graves. Unlike the rest, this one was overwhelmed with cards, candles, postcards and fresh flowers. Sally looked morose. The American family were laughing and smiling like they were at the fair; all they needed was candy floss and balloon animals. Sally turned to me, leaning into my ear.

'Everyone who loved these people, have now all gone for sure,' she mourned.

'The only ones who come here now are the tourists, and we're really no better than that.'

She went to turn back.

'Hey buddy!' I heard a Midwest accent.

It was the fattest of the Americans hollering at me in his green tracksuit bottoms, bumbag and baseball cap.

'Take our picture,' he said.

He placed a camera firmly in my hands as the rest of the family began to assemble in front of the grave. Sally looked removed. I held the disposable up to my eye. The herd said 'cheese' unprompted as I fanned my thumb across the wheel, winding the entire rest of the film into the cassette; tilting the lens towards the ground, capturing only their fat ankles. I took her hand as we walked back down the path; the joyful laughter faded away.

29

Sally had asked her dad for some money to book an earlier ticket; by the time we had got to the Gare du Nord, she had everything sorted out. The station was crowded as indifferent commuters shouldered through the hall. When it finally came to it, I said nothing, and just waited for the impact of her leaving. A security guard in orange hi vis and a matching baton glared at me from the side. Sally just looked done. She turned and headed towards the escalator to the second floor, for London Eurostar departures; I lingered to see if she would look back, but she just kept true, her shoulders hunched a little; another sight to haunt me; she never looked around, and with that there went the back of her head, bobbing away in a sea of faces.

30

A short walk from the station and I came across Le Cristal-Bar again, still at 35 Rue Louis Blanc. The bar girl serving had mousy hair and a real air of fuckoffness about her. While making my bloody mary, she took a sip from a straw and winced before adding several more fingers of vodka. She told me her favourite place was at the top of Parc de Belleville. It was back in the 20th Arrondissement, right by Père Lachaise, so I already knew how to get there.

31

I was afraid that with any genuine happiness came the capacity for its loss and in knowing that fact I would be prevented from ever truly living. The hill to the top of Belleville was gradual and sickening. Through the park the birds sang, and as I climbed the steps, my breath got heavier. The sky had remained grey and the light was hard. At the summit was a decrepit looking concrete building with a pavilion and a viewing platform. A wheatpasting of a pug with an orange crayon in its mouth was plastered over one of the graffitied pillars. On the dog was written: 'Love is the answer'. I walked over to the railing. A battered mosaic detailed a panoramic guide of the visible landmarks. From left to right was the Bibliothèque Mitterrand, then L'église Saint-Ambroise, Tour Jussieu, Sorbonne, and the Panthéon. After that, the rest of the sites were covered in bird shit and impossible to make out. Far out in the skyline, a solitary tower stood tall; two pin prick lights flickered irregularly over the canopy and pincered in the smog.

End